Santa is coming to Massachusetts

Written by Steve Smallman
Illustrated by Robert Dunn and Jerry Pyke
Designed by Sarah Allen

Published by Sourcebooks Jabberwocky, an imprint of Sourcebooks, Inc.
P.O. Box 4410, Naperville, Illinois 60567-4410
(630) 961-3900
Fax: (630) 961-2168
www.jabberwockykids.com

Library of Congress Cataloging-in-Publication data is on file with the publisher.

Source of Production: Leo Paper Products, Guangdong Province, China
Date of Production: April 2014
Run Number: HTW_PO170314
Printed and bound in China
LEO 10 9 8 7 6 5 4 3 2 1

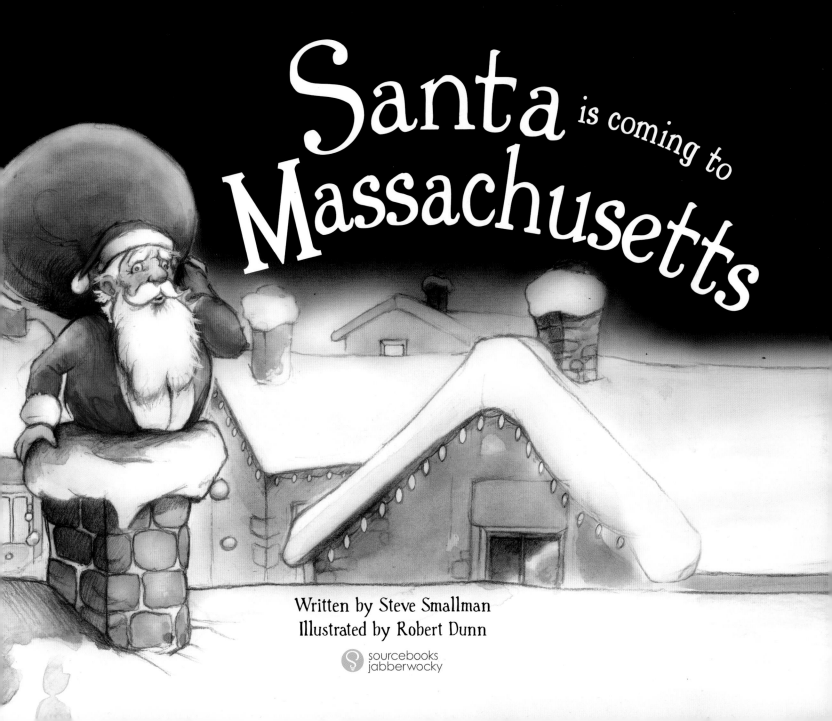

Santa is coming to Massachusetts

Written by Steve Smallman
Illustrated by Robert Dunn

sourcebooks
jabberwocky

"Well?"

boomed Santa. "Have all the children of **Massachusetts** been good this year?"

"Well...uh...mostly," answered the little old elf, as he bustled across the busy workshop to Santa's desk.

Santa peered down at the elf from behind the tall, teetering piles of letters that the children from Massachusetts had sent him.

"Mostly?" asked Santa, looking over the top of his glasses.

"Yes...but they've all been **especially** good in the last few days!" said the elf.

"Jolly good!" chuckled Santa.
"Then we'd better get their presents loaded up!"

Even though the sack of presents was

really, really big

and the elves were **really, really** small,

they seemed to have no trouble loading it onto Santa's sleigh.
Though how they managed to fit such a big sack into one little sleigh
even they didn't know. But somehow they did.

"Splendid!" boomed Santa. "We're ready to go!"

"Er...not quite, Santa," said the little old elf. "One of our reindeer is missing!"

"Missing?

Which reindeer is missing?" asked Santa.

"The youngest one, Santa," said the elf. "It's his first flight tonight. I've called him and called him, but..."

Just then, a young reindeer strolled up, munching on a large carrot.

"where have you been?"

asked Santa.

But the youngest reindeer was crunching so loudly that it was no wonder he hadn't heard the little old elf calling.

"Oh well, never mind," said Santa, giving the reindeer a little wink. He took out his Santa-nav and tapped in the coordinates for Massachusetts. **"This will guide us to Massachusetts in no time."**

Crunch!
Crunch!
Crunch!

With a flick of the reins and a jerk of the harness, off they went, racing through the sky.

"Ho, ho, ho!"

laughed Santa.

"We'll soon have these presents delivered to the Bay State!"

Santa's sleigh flew through the starry night, heading south across the Arctic Ocean. On they flew, in the crisp, wintry air, crossing over Canada. In the wink of an eye, the sleigh was flying above New England.

The youngest reindeer was very excited. He had never been away from the North Pole before.

They had just crossed Mount Greylock
when, suddenly, they ran into a blizzard.
Snowflakes whirled around the sleigh.

They couldn't see a thing!

The youngest reindeer was getting a bit worried,
but Santa didn't seem concerned.

"In two miles..."

said the Santa-nav in a bossy lady's voice,

"...keep left at the next star."

"But, ma'am," Santa blustered, "I can't see any stars in all this snow!"

Soon they were

hopelessly lost!

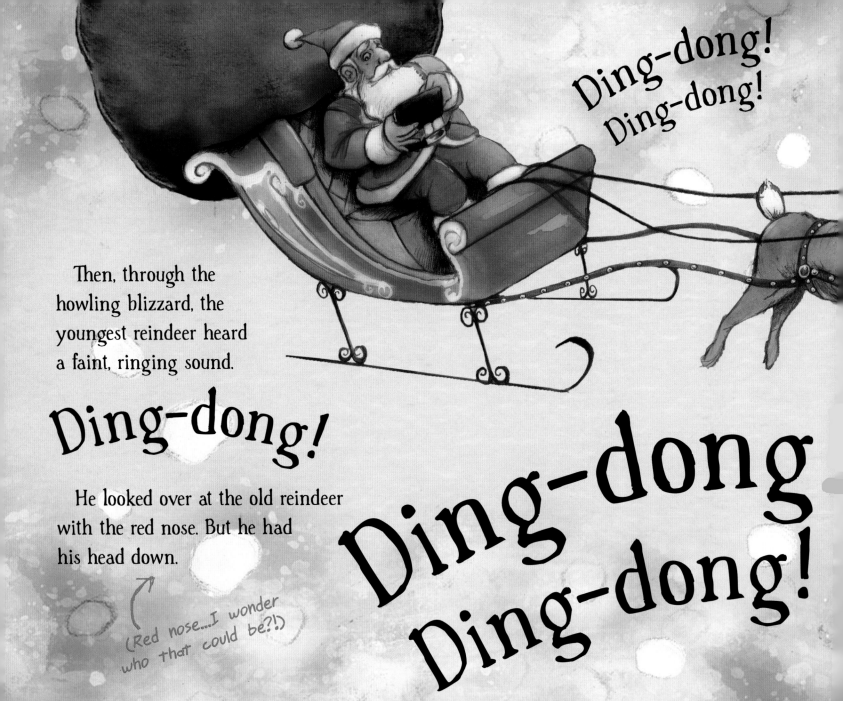

Ding-dong!
Ding-dong!

Then, through the
howling blizzard, the
youngest reindeer heard
a faint, ringing sound.

Ding-dong!

He looked over at the old reindeer
with the red nose. But he had
his head down.

(Red nose...I wonder
who that could be?!)

Ding-dong
Ding-dong!

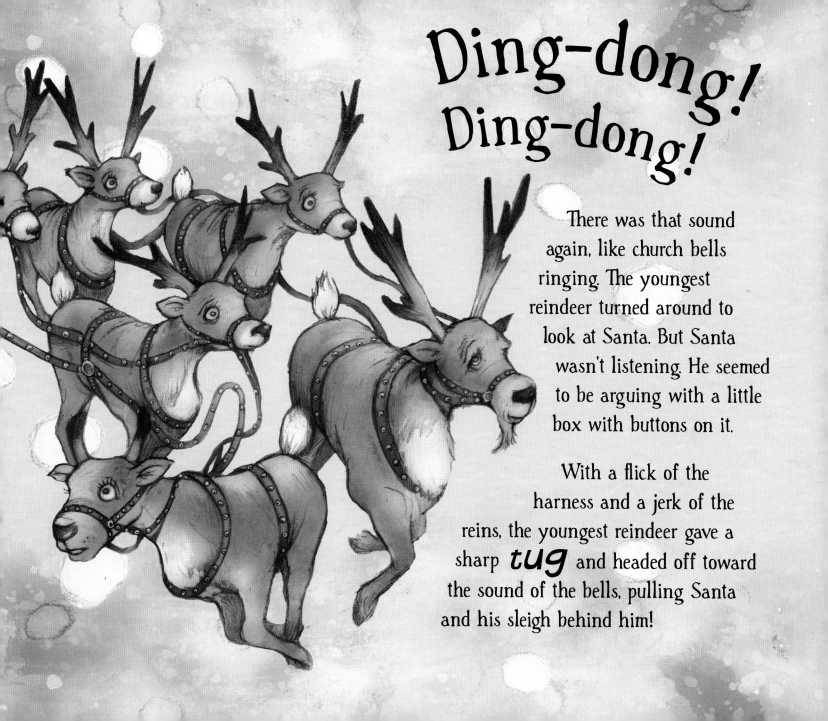

Ding-dong!
Ding-dong!

There was that sound
again, like church bells
ringing. The youngest
reindeer turned around to
look at Santa. But Santa
wasn't listening. He seemed
to be arguing with a little
box with buttons on it.

With a flick of the
harness and a jerk of the
reins, the youngest reindeer gave a
sharp *tug* and headed off toward
the sound of the bells, pulling Santa
and his sleigh behind him!

"Whoa!"

cried Santa, pulling his hat straight.
"What's going on?" Then, to his surprise,
he heard the ringing sound.

"Well done, young reindeer!" he shouted cheerfully,
"It must be the bells of the First Congregational Church
in Worcester! Don't worry, children, Santa is coming!"

Then, suddenly...

CRUNCH!

The sleigh hit something as it plummeted through the snow clouds. **"You have arrived!"** said the Santa-nav unhelpfully.

Finally, when the snow had died down and the clouds parted, Santa discovered exactly where they were...

...stuck, right at the very top of a **Christmas tree near the Worcester Common Oval.**

"Everybody, PULL!"

The reindeer *pulled* with all their might until,
at last, with a screeching noise, the sleigh scraped clear
of the Christmas tree and Santa steered them safely
over Worcester City Hall, past the Worcester Historical
Museum, above Becker College, and down into Elm Park.

Luckily, there was
no real damage
done, but the packages
had all been jumbled
up. Santa quickly put the
presents back in order.

"All right," said Santa. "Thanks
to this young reindeer, I know
where we are now. Don't worry, children,

Santa is coming!"

Santa drove his sleigh expertly from rooftop to rooftop all over Massachusetts, popping in and out of chimneys as fast as he could go.

(Which was pretty fast for a chubby fellow!)

There were big chimneys in Nantucket, and small chimneys in Amherst. He squeezed down thin chimneys in New Bedford, and plummeted down fat chimneys in Somerville.

The youngest reindeer
was amazed at how quickly
they went. Santa never seemed to get
tired at all! And it looked like
the children of Massachusetts were
going to be very lucky this year!
But the youngest reindeer was
starting to feel a bit weary,
and quite hungry too!

He piled them under the Christmas trees and carefully filled up the stockings with surprises.

In house after house, Santa delved inside his sack for packages of every shape and size.

Santa took a little bite out of each cookie, a tiny sip of milk, wiped his beard, and popped the carrots into his sack.

In house after house, the good children of Massachusetts had left out a large plate of cookies, a small glass of milk, and a big, crunchy carrot.

From Boston to Brockton, from Pittsfield to Springfield, from Cambridge to Concord, from Lowell to Lawrence, and ALL the places in between, Santa and his sleigh visited every house in Massachusetts.

Santa delivered presents to Abigail, Addison, Aiden, Alexander, Andrew, Ava...the list went on and on! ...Violet, Wyatt, Xavier, Zachary, Zoe, Zybil.

(Zybil? Surely that must be a spelling mistake!)

FENWAY PARK

Finally, Santa had delivered the last present on his long Massachusetts list.

"Great moons and stars!" sighed Santa. "It's past midnight and my sack seems as heavy as ever! I hope I haven't forgotten anyone."

Santa opened his sack to check...but it was full of juicy, crunchy carrots!

Santa divided the carrots among all the reindeer.
"Good job!" he said, patting the youngest reindeer gently on the nose.

But the youngest reindeer didn't hear him...he was too busy munching!

Then it was time to set off for home. Santa reset his Santa-nav once more
to the North Pole, and soon they were speeding past the Berkshires, over Walden
Pond, above Salem, and out over Ipswich Bay through the crisp, starry night.